Anonymous

The Young Lady's Oracle

A Fireside Amusement

Anonymous

The Young Lady's Oracle
A Fireside Amusement

ISBN/EAN: 9783337119676

Printed in Europe, USA, Canada, Australia, Japan

Cover: Foto ©Andreas Hilbeck / pixelio.de

More available books at **www.hansebooks.com**

THE

YOUNG LADY'S ORACLE:

A Fireside Amusement.

NEW YORK:

PUBLISHED BY JAMES MILLER,

(SUCCESSOR TO C. S. FRANCIS & CO),

522 BROADWAY.

1863.

HOW TO CONSULT THE ORACLE.

THE mode of consulting the Oracle is extremely simple. The Card, which will be found at the end of the volume, having been cut into separate pieces, each containing a single number (Nos. 3 to 18), the pieces are to be deposited in a reticule or other convenient receptacle, so that the drawer may choose at random without being able to see the number chosen. The person who wishes to consult the Oracle having selected the question (pp. vii – xii) to which she wishes a reply, then withdraws one of the cards from the reticule, which gives the answer to her question.

Thus, for example, supposing the First question to be the one selected — "SHALL I BE

MARRIED SOON?" and that the card which she has withdrawn is No. 17, the answer will be readily found as follows : —

Turn to the *Table of Answers* (pp. xiii – xvi), and in the first column you will find the number of the Question to which a reply is required, (1), and in the top line the number of the Card selected (17) : at the point of intersection of these two lines you will find 6, which indicates the page containing the answer. Thus turning to page 6, we find the reply of the Oracle No. 17 is — "YES, TO YOUR DARK ADMIRER."

QUESTIONS.

1. Shall I be married soon?
2. Shall I have what they've promised me?
3. Is my love well placed?
4. Who is my rival?
5. Where will my folly lead me?
6. Shall I have children?
7. Will my husband love me?
8. Shall I soon go to a ball?
9. Is my secret well kept?
10. Shall I make it up with him?
11. Does he not play me false?

12. What is wisdom in women?

13. Will my husband be rich?

14. How shall I retain all my lovers?

15. Should I marry?

16. Shall I fascinate him?

17. May I believe what he says?

18. What will be my greatest fault?

19. Shall I accept his proposal?

20. Is my dress becoming?

21. When shall I cease to weep?

22. Shall I write to him?

23. Should I forgive him?

24. Shall I succeed in my undertaking?

25. Shall I be lucky at play?

26. When will he return?

27. Shall I keep the appointment?

28. Does he love me sincerely?

29. Shall I go into the country?

30. Will my wishes be accomplished?

31. What is he doing?

32. What will be my fate?

33. Is he discreet?

34. Shall I be a widow?

35. Which shall I take — the dark or the light [one?

36. Will he come?

37. Will my husband be young?

38. Oracle! am I pretty?

39. When shall I die?

40. Must I be unkind?

41. How shall I secure his love?

42. When will old age begin with me?

43. How long will this intrigue last?

44. Are all husbands the same ?

45. What is the happiest state ?

46. Will my tricks be found out ?

47. Shall I marry him I love ?

48. Shall I quarrel with him ?

49. Will he write to me ?

50. Will my family approve of my choice ?

51. Shall I have good news ?

52. Shall I give him hopes ?

53. What does the world think of me ?

54. Should I alter my conduct ?

55. Oracle ! shall I soon have a legacy ?

56. Whence comes my melancholy ?

57. How shall I silence scandal ?

58. Oracle ! what is love ?

59. Should I be fickle ?

60. Shall I have a soldier for a lover?

61. Am I not taking an imprudent step?

62. Oracle! what is life?

63. How shall I remove my annoyances?

64. Shall I be robbed?

65. Should I not profit by my youth?

66. Shall I lose my cause?

67. What is a good husband?

68. Should I keep my promise?

69. Shall I tell him my secret?

70. What is wisdom?

71. What is my principal defect?

72. Where is he?

73. Does gold give happiness?

74. Am I clever?

75. Are all women like me?

76. Shall I live in town or in the country?

77. Where shall I find pleasure?

78. Will my happiness be lasting?

79. Have I many enemies?

80. Which should I prefer — love or money?

TABLE OF ANSWERS.

Number of the Question.	3	4	5	6	7	8	9	10	11	12	13	14	15	16	17	18
1	16	21	26	31	36	41	46	51	56	61	66	71	76	1	6	11
2	17	22	27	32	37	42	47	52	57	62	67	72	77	2	7	12
3	18	23	28	33	38	43	48	53	58	63	68	73	78	3	8	13
4	19	24	29	34	39	44	49	54	59	64	69	74	79	4	9	14
5	20	25	30	35	40	45	50	55	60	65	70	75	80	5	10	15
6	21	26	31	36	41	46	51	56	61	66	71	76	1	6	11	16
7	22	27	32	37	42	47	52	57	62	67	72	77	2	7	12	17
8	23	28	33	38	43	48	53	58	63	68	73	78	3	8	13	18
9	24	29	34	39	44	49	54	59	64	69	74	79	4	9	14	19
10	25	30	35	40	45	50	55	60	65	70	75	80	5	10	15	20
11	26	31	36	41	46	51	56	61	66	71	76	1	6	11	16	21
12	27	32	37	42	47	52	57	62	67	72	77	2	7	12	17	22
13	28	33	38	43	48	53	58	63	68	73	78	3	8	13	18	23
14	29	34	39	44	49	54	59	64	69	74	79	4	9	14	19	24
15	30	35	40	45	50	55	60	65	70	75	80	5	10	15	20	25
16	31	36	41	46	51	56	61	66	71	76	1	6	11	16	21	26
17	32	37	42	47	52	57	62	67	72	77	2	7	12	17	22	27
18	33	38	43	48	53	58	63	68	73	78	3	8	13	18	23	28
19	34	39	44	49	54	59	64	69	74	79	4	9	14	19	24	29
20	35	40	45	50	55	60	65	70	75	80	5	10	15	20	25	30

Number of the Question.	3	4	5	6	7	8	9	10	11	12	13	14	15	16	17	18
21	36	41	46	51	56	61	66	71	76	1	6	11	16	21	26	31
22	37	42	47	52	57	62	67	72	77	2	7	12	17	22	27	32
23	38	43	48	53	58	63	68	73	78	3	8	13	18	23	28	33
24	39	44	49	54	59	64	69	74	79	4	9	14	19	24	29	34
25	40	45	50	55	60	65	70	75	80	5	10	15	20	25	30	35
26	41	46	51	56	61	66	71	76	1	6	11	16	21	26	31	36
27	42	47	52	57	62	67	72	77	2	7	12	17	22	27	32	37
28	43	48	53	58	63	68	73	78	3	8	13	18	23	28	33	38
29	44	49	54	59	64	69	74	79	4	9	14	19	24	29	34	39
30	45	50	55	60	65	70	75	80	5	10	15	20	25	30	35	40
31	46	51	56	61	66	71	76	1	6	11	16	21	26	31	36	41
32	47	52	57	62	67	72	77	2	7	12	17	22	27	32	37	42
33	48	53	58	63	68	73	78	3	8	13	18	23	28	33	38	43
34	49	54	59	64	69	74	79	4	9	14	19	24	29	34	39	44
35	50	55	60	65	70	75	80	5	10	15	20	25	30	35	40	45
36	51	56	61	66	71	76	1	6	11	16	21	26	31	36	41	46
37	52	57	62	67	72	77	2	7	12	17	22	27	32	37	42	47
38	53	58	63	68	73	78	3	8	13	18	23	28	33	38	43	48
39	54	59	64	69	74	79	4	9	14	19	24	29	34	39	44	49
40	55	60	65	70	75	80	5	10	15	20	25	30	35	40	45	50

Number of the Question	3	4	5	6	7	8	9	10	11	12	13	14	15	16	17	18
41	56	61	66	71	76	1	6	11	16	21	26	31	36	41	46	51
42	57	62	67	72	77	2	7	12	17	22	27	32	37	42	47	52
43	58	63	68	73	78	3	8	13	18	23	28	33	38	43	48	53
44	59	64	69	74	79	4	9	14	19	24	29	34	39	44	49	54
45	60	65	70	75	80	5	10	15	20	25	30	35	40	45	50	55
46	61	66	71	76	1	6	11	16	21	26	31	36	41	46	51	56
47	62	67	72	77	2	7	12	17	22	27	32	37	42	47	52	57
48	63	68	73	78	3	8	13	18	23	28	33	38	43	48	53	58
49	64	69	74	79	4	9	14	19	24	29	34	39	44	49	54	59
50	65	70	75	80	5	10	15	20	25	30	35	40	45	50	55	60
51	66	71	76	1	6	11	16	21	26	31	36	41	46	51	56	61
52	67	72	77	2	7	12	17	22	27	32	37	42	47	52	57	62
53	68	73	78	3	8	13	18	23	28	33	38	43	48	53	58	63
54	69	74	79	4	9	14	19	24	29	34	39	44	49	54	59	64
55	70	75	80	5	10	15	20	25	30	35	40	45	50	55	60	65
56	71	76	1	6	11	16	21	26	31	36	41	46	51	56	61	66
57	72	77	2	7	12	17	22	27	32	37	42	47	52	57	62	67
58	73	78	3	8	13	18	23	28	33	38	43	48	53	58	63	68
59	74	79	4	9	14	19	24	29	34	39	44	49	54	59	64	69
60	75	80	5	10	15	20	25	30	35	40	45	50	55	60	65	70

Number of the Question	3	4	5	6	7	8	9	10	11	12	13	14	15	16	17	18
61	76	1	6	11	16	21	26	31	36	41	46	51	56	61	66	71
62	77	2	7	12	17	22	27	32	37	42	47	52	57	62	67	72
63	78	3	8	13	18	23	28	33	38	43	48	53	58	63	68	73
64	79	4	9	14	19	24	29	34	39	44	49	54	59	64	69	74
65	80	5	10	15	20	25	30	35	40	45	50	55	60	65	70	75
66	1	6	11	16	21	26	31	36	41	46	51	56	61	66	71	76
67	2	7	12	17	22	27	32	37	42	47	52	57	62	67	72	77
68	3	8	13	18	23	28	33	38	43	48	53	58	63	68	73	78
69	4	9	14	19	24	29	34	39	44	49	54	59	64	69	74	79
70	5	10	15	20	25	30	35	40	45	50	55	60	65	70	75	80
71	6	11	16	21	26	31	36	41	46	51	56	61	66	71	76	1
72	7	12	17	22	27	32	37	42	47	52	57	62	67	72	77	2
73	8	13	18	23	28	33	38	43	48	53	58	63	68	73	78	3
74	9	14	19	24	29	34	39	44	49	54	59	64	69	74	79	4
75	10	15	20	25	30	35	40	45	50	55	60	65	70	75	80	5
76	11	16	21	26	31	36	41	46	51	56	61	66	71	76	1	6
77	12	17	22	27	32	37	42	47	52	57	62	67	72	77	2	7
78	13	18	23	28	33	38	43	48	53	58	63	68	73	78	3	8
79	14	19	24	29	34	39	44	49	54	59	64	69	74	79	4	9
80	15	20	25	30	35	40	45	50	55	60	65	70	75	80	5	10

ANSWERS.

3. Your cause is just; you will win.

4. Mind what you're about; you are watched.

5. Of his inconstancy.

6. They will give you much annoyance.

7. Your conduct will open people's eyes.

8. By the same means you employed with

9. Yes, in an hour. [others.

10. Nothing good.

11. The day of his arrival.

12. When it's all out of your head.

13. By a little more complaisance.

14. Oh! my dear, shamefully.

15. Yes, twins.

16. No; your faults are too well known.

17. Live where he is whom you love.

18. Idleness.

2

3. Yours.

4. A taper threatened with the extinguisher.

5. By out-talking the talkers.

6. It would make him too conceited.

7. Yes, if you persist.

8. Not before fifty years.

9. Yes, very young.

10. Nothing will come of it.

11. Go to your cost, if you must.

12. Imprudent!

13. He still says true,

14. What you, perhaps, will be, one day.

15. He need be very good.

16. Yes, despite delay.

17. Ask your light pet.

18. Whither his misdeeds have led him.

3. I see no obstacle.

4. You must pardon him.

5. A god who's as blind as a post.

6. Your ridiculous conceit makes you detestable.

7. You would do right, for he is deceiving you.

8. By a result you've no idea of.

9. Be assured to the contrary.

10. You may tell him all.

11. He'll love you for a month.

12. You would do well.

13. Your marriage.

14. No ; but he will become so.

15. Yes, at a bal-champêtre.

16. Yes, but what tears will it not cost you ?

17. I wish it may, but doubt it.

18. Yes, with something else into the bargain.

3. Wait a few months more.

4. Yes, to-night.

5. No, it would be wrong.

6. Yes, to avoid scandal.

7. Yes, what he does not at present think of.

8. Your mother will tell you.

9. Don't be uneasy.

10. No.

11. Go ; pleasure awaits you.

12. Yes, if you manage it well.

13. You would be wrong.

14. By affecting great simplicity.

15. Yes, my beauty.

16. An afflicted woman of nineteen.

17. Yes, but don't fear them.

18. Yes, the cleverest of women.

3. Your least quality.

4. Yes, but circumspectly.

5. Take my advice, and cut the trooper.

6. Don't hope it.

7. For several reasons he'll not be approved of.

8. None.

9. Sometimes ; not always.

10. Wait before you decide.

11. Your marriage will accomplish them.

12. Not always.

13. A little simplicity were better.

14. Wait ; you'll thank me for the advice.

15. Yes, but you'll be his dupe.

16. The most frightful misery.

17. Can you hesitate ?   Money.

18. Good gracious ! what would the men do.

3. Avarice.

4. Your adversary is powerful.

5. Yes, sometimes.

6. Of your jealousy.

7. No, my fair lady.

8. Be on your guard.

9. What, don't you know ?

10. He has elsewhere to go.

11. He is at the feet of your rival.

12. An hour before your marriage.

13. When you have what you desire.

14. By greater attention to dress.

15. He loves you too much for that.

16. Yes, and very charming ones.

17. Yes, to your dark admirer.

18. You'd die of ennui in the country.

3. Far hence.

4. He who is not jealous.

5. A thing you're very tenacious about.

6. Despise them.

7. That were too coquettish.

8. You can do as you like about it.

9. Your glass will tell you.

10. Somewhat on the turn.

11. Very brilliant.

12. It would be very dangerous.

13. No ; it would make him too conceited.

14. Listen, and you are lost.

15. The most resigned.

16. Yes, to death.

17. No doubt.

18. With work.

3. Not always.

4. Yes, if you can.

5. You must resign yourself to it.

6. A God guided by folly.

7. You are thought very amiable.

8. Do you desire it.

9. The wine is drawn ; it must be drunk.

10. You have been so, but are so no longer.

11. Could he do so ?

12. He is not mad enough for that.

13. He deserves it.

14. To refuse the offered match.

15. Yes, but silly.

16. Yes, to give a laugh to your enemies.

17. Calm your apprehensions.

18. No, unluckily.

3. Don't believe a word.

4. Don't be so foolish.

5. No, my love.

6. Your heart refuses.

7. Yes, but gradually.

8. Yes, but very seldom.

9. They are more or less amiable.

10. Await death without fear.

11. Marry, and I'll tell you.

12. No ; remain in town.

13. You will fail.

14. Yes, if it suits you.

15. By making no end of promises.

16. Not over well.

17. The prima donna of a foreign theatre.

18. As many as of friends.

3. Very few are like you.

4. What you have not, and never will have.

5. Yes, for they will pass rapidly.

6. Have you a fancy for the uniform?

7. Yes, from an uncle in America.

8. Hope.

9. Yours.

10. Why delay your happiness?

11. Your dark admirer is making a fool of you.

12. Yes, if you marry.

13. Play will be the ruin of you.

14. No, your tournure is not good.

15. Yes, to be happy.

16. Don't be such a fool.

17. To crime.

18. There's no longer a choice between the two.

3. In town, if you are mad.

4. Excessive jealousy.

5. The weight is on your side.

6. Yes, more than you imagine.

7. With the contempt he heaps on you.

8. Yes, very good.

9. What matters? It's too late for a remedy.

10. Don't affect ignorance.

11. Yes, when the sun is down.

12. He is thinking of you.

13. In a few days.

14. The day of your death.

15. What a ridiculous question!

16. No, and he is much in the wrong.

17. Yes, three boys.

18. Yes, for I believe you're in a hurry.

3. Nowhere; you're weary of everything.

4. He himself is far away, but his heart is with
                                            [you.
5. He that is destined for you.

6. A thing that every one fears to lose.

7. Your reputation may defy assault.

8. Why deceive him?

9. Don't doubt it.

10. The wrinkles in your face will tell you.

11. He's more than forty.

12. The horizon is very sombre.

13. Be on your guard; it's a snare.

14. You had better go and speak to him.

15. You may, without danger.

16. Nobody knows it.

17. No, he'll prefer the bottle.

18. Yes, on your birth-day.

3. Yes.

4. That's rare.

5. Yes, but calculate the future before you
6. You must be less ambitious.   [promise.

7. What you feel when you see your fair ad-
8. The women think you giddy.   [mirer.

9. Yes, unless you alter your conduct.

10. On that question the oracle is mute.

11. You have ceased to be so.

12. Yes, more than you.

13. He says so: you must believe him.

14. Yes, if he solicits pardon.

15. A too great love of change.

16. Very rich.

17. Yes, with one of your rivals.

18. Yes, but it cannot last.

3. Those you have are not formidable.

4. The spirit is ever about you.

5. Yes, but conceal nothing from him.

6. You will be robbed of your most precious

7. Yes, from time to time.   [jewel.

8. No doubt.

9. Yes, to tell you what you know already.

10. Yes, all equally simple.

11. Your life will be long and happy.

12. How curious you are!

13. It will involve you in great danger.

14. Don't be uneasy.

15. Yes, give yourself that satisfaction.

16. Don't attempt it ; you'd fail.

17. Quite enough, for its importance.

18. The rival of Madame Saqui.

3. Prefer fortune ; it is more durable.

4. Every one has'nt got your capacity.

5. The most precious of the Creator's gifts.

6. Yes, 'tis quite time.

7. You'll be fascinated with a horse-guardsman.

8. No, not before twenty.

9. Interest will guide you.

10. Prudence forbids me to tell you.

11. Yes, from time to time.

12. The light one does not love you.

13. It's impossible.

14. Yes, if you are tricky.

15. Yes, for ugliness well dressed seems almost [beauty.

16. Prefer celibacy.

17. Yes, very shortly.

18. Perhaps at the scaffold !

3. That will depend on yourself.

4. You will shine everywhere.

5 Coquetry.

6. Not if you tell the truth.

7. Yes, act with more reflection.

8. To see your rival triumph.

9. Don't let that disturb you.

10. They will, by a female friend. _

11. By promising everything.

12. Yes, in an instant.

13. He's at suicide !

14. Later than you imagine.

15. Very soon.

16. How simple you are !

17. Yes, but pardon him.

18. Yes, four girls.

3. No, you don't deserve it.

4. At the ball, for that's your passion.

5. With your enemy.

6. A very rare thing.

7. To some a burden.

8. They are so true, 'tis difficult.

9. It would be too much encouragement for him.

10. Your efforts are futile.

11. You are close upon your autumn.

12. It's very doubtful.

13. It will be terrible.

14. Imprudent! you would be undone.

15. He would show your letter to your enemies.

16. What does he say to you?

17. The most *charitable.*

18. Yes, far too much.

3. Yes, no doubt.

4. As your youth.

5. That depends on circumstances.

6. Not if you would remain virtuous.

7. Renounce your projects.

8. What you would inspire.

9. Your conduct is censured.

10. Your reputation requires it.

11. Very bad.

12. Yes, with a masque.

13. Like the Phrygian reeds.

14. I don't believe it.

15. It would save his life.

16. To tell him your secret.

17. Yes, rich and amiable.

18. You will be invited, but don't go.

3. What matters it to you? You need not fear.

4. They're about you on all sides.

5. If you were, you would not ask the question.

6. No, he would abandon you.

7. Yes, by your fair admirer.

8. What an absurd question !

9. Yes, out of courtesy.

10. Yes, to make fun of you.

11. There's little variety in species.

12. The hour of your death has not struck.

13. If you are married, don't wish it.

14. Yes, but don't remain there long.

15. Yes, despite envy.

16. No ; give a civil refusal.

17. By using coquetry.

18. Yes, despite its weight.

3. To repentance.

4. Love, if sincere, is preferable.

5. What would become of the husbands?

6. What you'll never acquire.

7. Can you ask the question!

8. An artilleryman will take your heart by

9. Yes, but others will profit by it. [assault.

10. You've made a wretched choice.

11. You'll soon know.

12. By and by.

13. The dark one will be rich.

14. Yes, I assure you.

15. If you're wise, you'll not play.

16. It does not set you off.

17. No, not yet.

18. Yes, if you make the first advance.

3. Infinitely.

4. Before long, you'll be Mrs. — you know who.

5. In the country you'll be more of your own

6. Pride.   [mistress.

7. Not, if you get a good lawyer.

8. Reassure yourself; they are not so.

9. Things the most frivolous.

10. They cannot fail to be so.

11. Yes, you'll have that vexation.

12. By conforming to his wishes.

13. Perhaps this evening.

14. His will.

15. Midsummer-day

16. When you're a little less perverse.

17. By your virtues.

18. Yes, and he is quite in the right.

3. Yes, if your conduct is irreproachable.

4. Yes, if you are discreet.

5. At Blind-man's Buff.

6. At a ball, with a black-eyed girl.

7. Marry, and you'll know.

8. A comedy in several acts.

9. Your marriage will silence them.

10. Yes, but be cautious.

11. Fortunately, no.

12. If I were to tell you, you'd hate me.

13. He'll be between 20 and 60.

14. It will be mixed flowers and thorns.

15. Your search would be fruitless.

16. Never write, or you are lost.

17. Yes, but not all.

18. You, my fair lady.

3. Prepare yourself.

4. Be assured to the contrary.

5. Yes, a month and more.

6. Yes, that of ambition.

7. No, it would undo you.

8. Be less jealous, and you will be happy.

9. A thing that has no actual existence.

10. You are criticized indulgently.

11. Yes, to silence chatter.

12. Very well.

13. Yes, to sketch.

14. Yes, very discreet.

15. He must have known you very little.

16. Forgiveness is a duty.

17. Ignorance on the point is bliss.

18. Yes, in hope.

3. 'Twas known long ago.

4. You know as well as I.

5. You've more of them than of friends.

6. Yes, but not very modest.

7. Do you think of it?

8. Yes, if you don't take care.

9. Yes, if you can.

10. Several reasons compel you to it.

11. What would he say to you?

12. No, far from it.

13. The day when you cease to live.

14. Alas! no.

15. Yes, in a few days.

16. No, my dear.

17. Yes, without hesitation.

18. 'Tis a trifle.

3. He loves you so dearly.

4. To your ruin.

5. That's as it may happen.

6. Yés, all equally artificial.

7. The greatest ornament of your sex.

8. Yes, but indifferently.

9. Yes, a lancer.

10. No, to your great regret.

11. Yes, if you manage it skilfully.

12. He can't have any of them.

13. You are too old.

14. Take both of them.

15. They will be, sooner or later.

16. At times you will be happy.

17. She's too old-fashioned.

18. Yes, to repair your fault.

3. Could he do otherwise?

4. More than you want.

5. Thirty years hence.

6. In town, if you like noisy pleasures.

7. Vanity.

8. No, and his loss will ruin you.

9. Yes, but no one observes it.

10. A desire you cannot satisfy.

11. Much better than the last.

12. Yes, by your husband.

13. By getting rid of your rivals.

14. Yes, to break with you.

15. He is fighting a duel for you.

16. To-morrow morning.

17. Soon, if you alter your conduct.

18. The sight of you alone will charm him.

3. An unknown masterpiece.

4. No, never !

5. Yes, but you won't be satisfied with it.

6. You could attain them.

7. I am too discreet to say.

8. The most docile to his dear rib.

9. An anecdote more or less long.

10. By correcting your bad habits.

11. I permit you.

12. Yes, if you wish it.

13. Sooner than you like.

14. He'll be much younger than you.

15. What shall I say to you ?

16. Your honor forbids it.

17. Yes, but be brief.

18. It would occasion you much evil.

3. Is it necessary for your happiness?

4. Yes, to embroider there.

5. There might be a more fitting object.

6. Not very long.

7. Ask Elwes, the miser.

8. That would involve over obligation.

9. You must yield to his entreaties.

10. A thing that passes away with time.

11. They think you absurdly affected.

12. Pretend to break it off.

13. By a tiff.

14. Yes, when you're painted.

15. A secret is always a great burden to him.

16. Yes, with all his man's heart.

17. Don't be insensible to his tears.

18. To be over prudish with him.

3. Coquette! isn't one enough for you?

4. Everybody knows it.

5. If I were to tell you, you'd be furious.

6. Yes, and very inveterately.

7. Candidly, I think not.

8. Which?

9. Reassure yourself; you'll not be so.

10. Yes, but only in love.

11. It's time, my beauty.

12. Yes, to make you a thousand promises.

13. Yes, all the same.

14. Never; you are immortal

15. Yes, after being married 75 years.

16. Yes, in a large company.

17. Just at the apparent point of success you'll

18. Yes, if you think him sincere. [fail.

3. Ask your heart.

4. Can he live without you ?

5. To premature old age.

6. You'll be happy with neither of them.

7. All have not your excellencies.

8. A very rare virtue.

9. Do as you please.

10. Soldiers are always changing quarters.

11. Imprudent woman ! What do you seek ?

12. She could not but approve of him.

13. Marriage.

14. Why martyrize him ?

15. Neither of them.

16. No, they are too ambitious.

17. You'll lose your patrimony by it.

18. She makes you look like a grisette.

3. By a better character.

4. Don't seek to know.

5. Yes, but very little.

6. I doubt it.

7. To the most retired rurality.

8. The love of pleasure.

9. Can you doubt it?

10. Go, and fear nothing.

11. Your lady friends will tell you.

12. They won't be so bad as all that.

13. Yes, if you slight my counsels.

14. Ask your mother.

15. He'll come to dine with you.

16. There's a plot hatching against you.

17. Don't hope to see him again.

18. When you have replaced him.

3. Not, if you would continue discreet.

4. The most discreet.

5. Yes, for you deserve it.

6. Perhaps.

7. This evening, you'll not repeat that question.

8. He is revelling.

9. There are none left in France.

10. A field that Death is always reaping.

11. Be resigned ; the thing is impossible.

12. Yes, but be on your guard.

13. Many obstacles will debar you.

14. She will begin very soon.

15. Young enough to think you old.

16. What inquisitiveness ?   I won't tell you.

17. Go there with a companion.

18. Yes, but don't sign anything.

3. That which you will commit this evening.

4. You occupy yourself with very futile things.

5. Yes, but be masqued.

6. Never mind; go on with it.

7. It won't last at all long.

8. Folly says, yes; wisdom, no.

9. The wine is drawn; it must be drunk.

10. Nothing; they are chimerical.

11. Sometimes a tragedy.

12. People laugh at your pride.

13. Where would you find another so good?

14. It will end happily.

15. You would be so, were you not so plain.

16. No, and he's proud of it.

17. Yes, for he thinks you prudent.

18. No, his fault is unpardonable.

3. Why not ?

4. Impossible ; you're not clever enough.

5. It's too heavy to keep.

6. What a question !   You have none.

7. Only female enemies.

8. You might be a little more so.

9. Yes, if you are penitent.

10. It's very possible.

11. Constancy rather belongs to your time of life.

12. No, go on.

13. Yes, to reproach you.

14. Yes, all equally stupid.

15. At past eighty.

16. Yes, but at a very advanced age.

17. My child, I think not.

18. Yes, if you follow the right path.

3. Everything fits you admirably.

4. No, not if you would be happy.

5. You would do wrong.

6. It's of no use to tell you.

7. Prefer love, and fortune will follow.

8. Yes, most of them.

9. A very frail thing.

10. You ask too late ; 'tis past.

11. Yes, a colonel of infantry.

12. You'll soon know.

13. Could they hesitate?

14. The state in which one lives free.

15. No, you are not enough of an actress.

16. Take the dark one.

17. No, to your great annoyance.

18. Luck will be various.

3. Never !

4. By greater modesty.

5. Coward ! Can you suspect ?

6. I'll tell you to-morrow, if you'll be discreet.

7. No, for you are too flighty.

8. In town, till you're thirty.

9. The being too flighty.

10. A false witness will lose it for you.

11. When they are, I'll tell you.

12. It would be too long a story.

13. You shall have excellent.

14. You must expect it.

15. By conforming to his humor.

16. Yes, since he has promised you.

17. He forgets you in the smoke of his cigar.

18. To-morrow, or never.

3. Avoid it most carefully.

4. No, he is deceiving you.

5. The husband's philosopher's stone.

6. Yes, a little.

7. Don't expect it any longer.

8. In the society you adorn.

9. He's running about the country.

10. The least wilful.

11. A journey full of accidents.

12. By steady coolness and perseverance.

13. 'Tis useless.

14. Impossible; he loves another.

15. Shortly.

16. Yes, rich, young, and amiable.

17. It will be unhappy.

18. Yes, if you can rely upon yourself.

3. Not yet; it's too soon.

4. That of slighting my counsel.

5. Yes, but you'll ruin him.

6. Yes, to meet your rival there.

7. No, for it's behind time.

8. No, by your own fault.

9. Yes, if you make good use of it.

10. No, my dear.

11. You must renounce the world.

12. A boy you must mistrust.

13. A very bad one.

14. Yes, break with him.

15. Very well, if you manage it skilfully.

16. An ill mind in a beautiful frame.

17. He is so, and always will be so.

18. Yes, but it will not be eternal.

3. You will encounter many obstacles.

4. Yes, but not for a month.

                          [person !

5. What a question from such a knowing

6. In future, bestow your confidence better.

7. A prettier woman than yourself.

8. Yes, more than you think.

9. You will never have that happiness.

10. It's needless ; he knows it.

11. Not if you are prudent.

12. Very seldom.

13. Yes, if you are able.

14. Impossible; he can't write.

15. Yes ; yours alone is an exception.

16. Before 1950.

17. Unluckily, no.

18. Yes, next spring.

3. Play, but in moderation.

4. That's as it may be thought.

5. Take good care of that; you're too flighty.

6. Get another; he'll not come back.

7. To a return to proper conduct.

8. Prefer fortune; so your ambition dictates.

9. That would be a calamity.

10. A path difficult to pursue.

11. Yes, for pleasure befits your age.

12. With a voltigeur, you'd have many campaigns to make.

13. A relation will leave you a legacy.

14. No, my love; he won't be sanctioned.

15. The state of innocence.

16. Yes, for a few days.

17. Take the fair one.

18. Yes, to stop your tears.

3. Too soon,

4. When you're more steady.

5. By somewhat less prudery.

6. Continue in your ignorance.

7. There's every probability.

8. Don't rely upon it.

9. I advise you to live in town.

10. I don't know one you have.

11. A mysterious personage will gain it for you.

12. No, not at all.

13. Can't you guess.

14. No, unluckily.

15. Not if you can be circumspect.

16. By making him no end of promises.

17. No, for he has ceased to love you.

18. Mischief.

3. Yes, if you like.

4. That would be improper.

5. Believe him, he is sincere.

6. A treasure not to be found.

7. Not much.

8. You are not likely to obtain it.

9. In your boudoir.

10. At the feet of his new love.

11. The greatest fool.

12. A mixture of honey and vinegar.

13. By avoiding that which causes it.

14. Yes, but don't be too yielding.

15. No, for I refuse my sanction.

16. Fear not : you are still young.

17. He will be old, poor, and cross.

18. Most happy.

3. Do not seek to know.

4. That will depend upon his conduct.

5. You are too prudent to commit any.

6. If he were rich, he would not marry you.

7. Yes, but don't give yourself up to it.

8. Yes, there is ample return.

9. You have many evils to undergo.

10. It were folly to believe it.

11. Take my advice ; don't keep it.

12. You must quit town.

13. A skilful archer.

14. They think you rather silly.

15. With which ?

16. In a duel, in which your lover will be killed.

17. Yes, but you think too much of it.

18. Discretion is his sole virtue.

3. Yes, next month.

4. Don't expect it.

5. That would be a folly.

6. By granting everything.

7. It could not be better placed.

8. A little simple thing of forty!

9. Be on your guard; they are numerous.

10. Your wit equals your beauty.

11. Yes, if you've courage enough.

12. No, but you will rob — hearts.

13. You may, till you're thirty.

14. Yes, if you want to get a husband.

15. Why should he write to you?

16. Women would be too much to be pitied.

17. Before a hundred years.

18. My dear friend, I quite despair of it.

3. Yes, all, except one.

4. It will be the making of your fortune.

5. No, you carry it so badly.

6. Marriage is worse than the plague.

7. Yes, if you can bring him back to you.

8. Alas ! Don't you foresee ?

9. Love.

10. Few are so inconstant.

11. A vessel that is often wrecked.

12. Yes, but dread the consequences.

13. Yes, a hussar.

14. Whence should it come to you?

15. Be happy; they approve it.

16. For you, a nunnery.

17. Yes, if you can.

18. The dark one will be more constant.

3. He forgets you.

4. He will be to-morrow at your feet.

5. When you are married.

6. By a few little attentions.

7. You must make up your mind to it.

8. Yes, but only two.

9. Don't be in such a hurry.

10. In the country you'll find happiness.

11. Backbiting.

12. Yes, but unjustly.

13. They can't be more so.

14. From absurd fears.

15. Yes, but they will be false.

16. Don't let that fear annoy you.

17. By pretending to love some one else. [time.

18. Don't wait for him; 'twould be losing your

3. It will be like the past.

4. What would you do there?

5. Why not?

6. You cannot too thoroughly mistrust him.

7. She who does not resemble you.

8. Assuredly.

9. Be sure of it.

10. What a curious question!

11. With his marchioness.

12. The most credulous.

13. A bitter narcotic plant.

14. By less equivocal conduct.

15. Yes, but very little.

16. Yes, despite the envious.

17. People at your age don't think of that.

18. Yes, but very ugly.

3. Indifferently.

4. In his heart he detests you.

5. He is too ungrateful.

6. The yielding too readily.

7. Yes, richer than you.

8. Could there be one without you ?

9. It were impossible to be better.

10. Yes, if you can moderate your pleasures.

11. Gold is a chimera.

12. You cannot do otherwise.

13. Marry.

14. The most painful of maladies.

15. People laugh at your pretension.

16. Yes, if you have the courage.

17. By a marriage and a baptism.

18. Not so much so as you think.

3. Never.

4. Why wish it?

5. Yes, despite all obstacles.

6. He does not love you enough.

7. By an intrigue skilfully conducted.

8. Don't be alarmed.

9. A very prudent woman.

10. Their number is appalling.

11. You were, but are so no longer.

12. No, he'd tell everybody.

13. That would not be easy.

14. No, for that is the act of a madwoman.

15. Yes, for your youth is passing away.

16. Perhaps.

17. Yes, all bad fellows alike.

18. At your age, you need not think of that.

3. Take the most fashionable.

4. Their accomplishment will cost you dear.

5. That passion will be your destruction.

6. Charmingly.

7. Yes, but no sooner than you need.

8. He no longer thinks of you.

9. In a few years you will know.

10. I have said it : gold does not give happiness.

11. None are so prudish.

12. The enemy of folly.

13. Yes, for it won't last long.

14. Your husband will be a citizen-soldier.

15. You will have two.

16. Yes, I promise you.

17. If you were in love, you would know.

18. You would only lose by it.

3. Yes, to-morrow.

4. Laughing at your constancy.

5. Not for three years to come.

6. This evening.

7. That's a question not to be asked, Madame.

8. What makes you think so.

9. Yes, several.

10. Yes, if you alter your conduct.

11. In town, you would ruin yourself.

12. Hypocrisy.

13. I much fear so.

14. Yes, very imprudent.

15. From a malady you seek in vain to cure.

16. They'll be neither good nor bad.

17. No, but make haste and reform.

18. Ask your companion.

3. Yes, too young for you.

4. It will be very fortunate.

5. Your heart should tell you.

6. 'Tis useless.

7. I don't advise it.

8. An imaginary object.

9. Not at all.

10. Alas, no.

11. In the country.

12. With a milliner.

13. A simple man.

14. A history too brief.

15. By skilful tactics.

16. Yes, if you would give him happiness.

17. I give you my consent.

18. At sixty you will still look young.

3. Yes, when you pout.

4. At times.

5. He knows you too well.

6. 'Tis too late.

7. Inconstancy.

8. You will know in a year.

9. Yes, to your cost.

10. Yes, but it will cost you dear.

11. Your happiness draws near its close.

12. Yes, the happiness of a miser.

13. A promise given, is due.

14. Despise them.

15. A story more or less long.

16. They think you somewhat backbiting.

17. Yes, for you begin to hate yourself.

18. In the loss of your reputation.

3. When your last hour is come.

4. To what purpose?

5. You find great pleasure there, then?

6. A trifle will stop you.

7. Yes, but later.

                                                        [it you.

8. You know your part: 'tis needless to teach

9. In future keep your secrets to yourself.

10. An Andalusian with small feet.

11. Yes, but you will overcome them all.

12. Sufficiently, for your position in the world.

13. That were the way to quarrel with him.

14. Yes, to your great satisfaction.

15. You are not skilful enough.

16. Yes, bid farewell to love.

17. Yes, but don't read his letter.

18. It were desirable.

3. Take good care to avoid that.

4. Take the most attentive.

5. No, to your misfortune.

6. Seldom.

7. You don't need it.

8. Yes, seize any opportunity.

9. A reconciliation is impossible.

10. I dare not tell you.

11. Love will be more agreeable to you.

12. It is not desirable.

13. A virtue that you don't practise.

14. Why not?

15. Yes, a half-pay.

16. Alas! who can tell?

17. Yes, for your happiness.

18. With you, to be a millionaire.

3. By making a slight advance.

4. Yes, if he has nowhere else to go.

5. He is waiting for you.

6. A letter from him will inform you.

7. Alas! who can foresee!

8. By your wit.

9. You would well deserve it.

10. Why not?

11. Many things prevent it.

12. In town you would be unhappy.

13. Pride.

14. It is certain that you will gain it.

15. Yes, very.

16. From too prolonged a fast.

17. They will afflict you.

18. You will never have that vexation.

3. At thirty, your hair will be gray.

4. Yes, young and amiable.

5. You will regret the past.

6. No doubt.

7. He would not answer you.

8. You would repent it.

9. What you never will be.

10. Yes, during the honeymoon.

11. I imagine you are waiting in vain.

12. Don't go in search of it; it will come of

13. At the feet of your rival.   [itself.

14. A blind man.

15. A thing easily lost.

16. There are a thousand ways.

17. Yes, in order to keep him.

18. What, marry such a man as that!

3. Don't you foresee?

4. They who say so are flatterers.

5. Don't confide in him at all.

6. Why not believe so?

7. Reflect before you do so.

8. To quarrel with him.

9. No; and it will be no harm.

10. Not so soon as you desire.

11. Indifferently.

12. Yes, if you are virtuous.

13. Alone, no.

14. What have you promised?

15. Tell me what causes your grief?

16. An idol that the whole world worships.

17. They consider you charming.

18. You would be wretched.

3. They are all equally tyrants.

4. On the last day of your existence.

5. Fortunately, no.

6. It is not quite the time.

7. Yes, but with difficulty.

8. Not yet ; it's too soon.

9. You are not sharp enough.

10. It's all about the town.

11. Your old friend.

12. More than you have adorers.

13. Far from it.

14. 'Tis no use ; somebody else will tell him.

15. Women of your age are not susceptible of

16. It would cost you too dear.   [it.

17. Ay, as soon as possible.

18. I doubt it.

3. Celibacy.

4. Not with him.

5. Pull straws for them.

6. Patience ; they will be so.

7. Often.

8. What a coquette you are !

9. Yes, and at once ; there's no time to lose.

10. I forbid it.

11. To a terrible trial.

12. Up to thirty, prefer love.

13. Yes, all equally coquettes.

14. The road to happiness.

15. Yes, but be prudent.

16. Save you from that !

17. How greedy ! Haven't you enough already ?

18. Yes, for it is excellent.

3. 'Tis in vain you seek to conceal them.

4. By making a great sacrifice.

5. It is very probable.

6. A very foolish thing.

7. Never : he is forsaking you.

8. Soon.

9. By sincere love.

10. Even if it were so ?

11. It's very doubtful.

12. Assuredly not.

13. In the country, if you're wise.

14. You have them all alike.

15. If I were the judge, you would lose.

16. Yes.

17. From over sensibility.

18. They will be very satisfactory.

3. Yes, but not without some trouble.

4. At a very advanced age.

5. In two months you will know.

6. You'll have many a shipwreck.

7. Can you help it?

8. Not now.

9. Yes, if he perseveres.

10. The most constant.

11. Be easy; he will adore you.

12. I'll tell you to-morrow.

13. At the play.

14. I dare not tell you.

15. See Mayhew's " Whom to Marry."

16. The vassal of death.

17. By address and perseverance.

18. Yes, to amuse him.

3. Yes, for a week.

4. In a great exposure.

5. Take a looking-glass.

6. Not over and above.

7. Yes, for a time.

8. Impossible.

9. Coquetry.

10. Enough to satisfy your frivolous tastes.

11. It is impossible.

12. So so.

13. Yes, from midday to midnight.

14. Seldom.

15. Yes, but not just yet.

16. Oh, there are a great many ways.

17. A slippery ground.

18. People laugh at your ignorance.

3. Yes, from time to time.

4. No, yours is not so good as the rest.

5. A long while hence.

6. You were much to be pitied.

7. Yes, if you like solitude.

8. Yes, in twenty years.

9 You would repent it.

10. Experience alone will teach you.

11. Your confidant is a great chatterer.

12. Don't seek to know.

13. Yes, many.

14. Enough to be pleasant.

15. Yes, if you can without blushing.

16. Be on your guard.

17. You can't, for a reason.

18. Yes, to procure oblivion of the past.

3. They would do wrong.

4. Widowhood.

5. As little as possible.

6. The fair one is too young.

7. Hope.

8. Sometimes.

9. Not enough to set you off.

10. Avoid that folly.

11. He is eager to make up for his ill conduct.

12. After lightning, thunder.

13. Prefer love to fortune.

14. Heaven preserve us from it!
                                          [us.
15. That which we lose when love comes upon

16. At your age women don't ask the question.

17. Neither drummer nor trumpeter.

18. Yes, when all your teeth are gone.

3. Very good.

4. How could it be otherwise ?

5. Patience ! Time will do it for you.

6. Don't expect him.

7. An infidelity.

8. Sunday, after morning service.

9. You have so many annoyances.

10. By consulting his tastes.

11. Yes, very often.

12. You need not hope it.

13. Not before sixty.

14. During the summer, in the country.

15. Indifference.

16. A mysterious person will gain it for you.

17. Hum ! Well, I don't say, no.

18. From your sadness.

3. Why not, if you love him?

4. Yes, but not for some years to come.

5. You are not young now.

6. Much older than yourself.

7. Your present conduct will make it miserable.

8. Can you hesitate?

9. Yes, if he is discreet.

10. Calm your apprehensions : he is sincere.

11. An unknown being.

12. I believe not.

13. You will know this evening.

14. You have it offered you in a thousand places.

15. You have no further business to know.

16. A middle-aged man.

17. A path between precipices.

18. What do you ask?

3. You are thought very clever.

4. Impossible : he is too fond of you.

5. In a great misfortune.

6. As an angel.

7. He told me your secret.

8. He adores you.

9. He would be too happy.

10. That of deceiving him.

11. Yes, but your follies will ruin him.

12. Not this year.

13. Hum! not over well.

14. Yes, if you are prudent.

15. Sometimes : not always.

16. Yes, but in secret.

17. Don't see him again.

18. The pastime of idiots.

3. Your position requires it.

4. Yes, to say nonsense to you.

5. What matters, since you cannot change.

6. Your question is indiscreet.

7. No, fortunately for you.

8. Yes, but come back soon.

9. It is too daring.

10. Yes, if you are mad.

11. Ask your friends.

12. Can you doubt it?

13. Your intimate friend.

14. Oh! and very terrible ones, too.

A 15. narrow escape from being an idiot. [ces.

16. If you do, I won't answer for the consequen-

17. Tell me your age, and I'll answer your

18. Believe me, you would do wrong. [question.

3. Yes, but it will occasion you many tears.

4. No, for she desires your happiness.

5. Youth.

6. You would repent it.

7. The dark one is too old.

8. Yes, in a few days.

9. You play too high.

10. Not so well as you think.

11. A fool would say yes : I say, no.

12. That will be difficult.

13. For everything except happiness.

14. Fortune is as nothing without love.

15. There are very few so grotesque.

16. What very few like at your age.

17. Yes, make the best of your time.

18. Soldiers are out of fashion.

3. From the absence of your beloved.

4. They will be very alarming.

5. Not if you manage adroitly.

6. I will tell you in his presence.

7. This evening, between eleven and twelve.

8. He is marrying another.

9. His absence will be extended.

10. The moment is not come.

11. By a return to prudence.

12. Not the least in the world.

13. Certainly.

14. Calm your impatience.

15. During the winter, in town.

16. Inconstancy.

17. Is any other result possible?

18. Yes, evidently.

3. You'll have a great deal to do.

4. Certainly : what do you risk ?

5. Your parents will oppose it.

6. What matters, you will always please.

7. He will be under eighty.

8. As prosperous as the present.

9. Yes, but change the place.

10. He would not read your letter.

11. No, he flatters you too much.

12. The least jealous.

13. Yes, but not for long.

14. Not now, but soon.

15. In noisy pleasures

16. Merrymaking.

17. A man who does not see very clearly.

18. Our treasure.

3. The tyrant of all hearts.

4. A very good one.

5. Yes, by your own fault.

6. In a scandalous quarrel.

7. You are told so often enough.

8. He could not be so.

9. Not altogether.

10. You would be his dupe.

11. It is committed ; 'tis too late to talk about it.

12. Don't doubt it.

13. The day of your marriage.

14. The future will tell you.

15. Yes, if you conduct yourself prudently.

16. That's as it may happen.

17. Wait ; the pear's not ripe.

18. Make it up with him.

3. You would do well to abstain from it.

4. Conscience should be your guide.

5. Yes, a letter as monotonous as himself.

6. Ask your friends.

7. Don't be uneasy.

8. You should not desire it.

9. Yes, soon.

10. Appearances are against you.

11. Do as you please ; he deceives you.

12. Be wily, and you'll succeed.

13. Far from it.

14. A rope dancer.

15. Enough to undo you.

16. Your face does not say so.

17. Your honor requires it.

18. You already are so.

3. Yes, a fickle Light-Dragoon.

4. Not soon, happily.

5. Don't hope it.

6. That depends on taste.

7. To what purpose?

8. The fair one is the more amiable.

9. Yes, in a few years.

10. At what game?

11. Can it be otherwise?

12. That would be an act of wisdom.

13. Don't hope it.

14. To a formidable result.

15. That depends on your age.

16. Can you presume it?

17. You will never know.

18. You consult me very late, my beauty.

3. Yes, they excite much talk.

4. From a love annoyance.

5. Yes, excellent.

6. They are so already.

7. Your heart should guide you.

8. Yes, but be cautious.

9. Why make yourself uneasy ?

10. Very soon.

11. When you have expiated your fault.

12. By somewhat less vanity.

13. He is more faithful than you.

14. No, unluckily.

15. No, you are not good-looking enough.

16. That depends on your fortune.

17. Gluttony.

18. You'll soon know.

3. A great drama.

4. It's of no use ; you won't succeed.

5. Yes, to fix him.

6. No, he'd make you unhappy.

7. Between nineteen and seventy.

8. He'll be older than you like.

9. Be more precise with your questions.

10. Yes, I permit it.

11. Would you venture.

12. No, he is making a fool of you.

13. A great problem.

14. Yes, if you are amiable.

15. Yes, if you yield.

16. In study.

17. Where you by no means think he is.

18. A friend of joy.

3. Forget him.

4. A boy who is the occasion of many follies.

5. They think you rather giddy.

6. Yes, and for ever.

7. By a mortal and mutual hatred.

8. You know well enough ; no.

9. Yes, but not enough.

10. Not yet.

11. His faults have been too great.

12. The not profiting by your youth.

13. No, but good.

14. Yes, but your fair admirer won't be there.

15. Yes, but —

16. Before long, it will all change.

17. Alone, it would not effect mine.

18. Nonsense, you don't mean it.

3. What should they rob you of?

4. Fear lest you repent it?

5. Yes, if you can.

6. Don't believe a word he writes.

7. They are all jealous alike.

8. Not to-day or to-morrow.

9. The oracle must be silent.

10. Alone! you would do wrong.

11. Hum! ha!

12. Can you hesitate?

13. By amiability.

14. Yes, very well.

15. An old girl of sixty.

16. Oh dear, many, many.

17. To silly questions, no reply.

18. Let him remain ignorant of your fault.

3. It would cost you many tears.

4. Yes, a lieutenant of dragoons.

5. Yes, but you'll soon dissipate it.

6. They will interpose obstacles.

7. That for you were riches.

8. Yes, if you would have him abandon you.

9. The fair one has wit.

10. Don't fear, they will be.

11. No, not even at the great game of all.

12. It is not fine enough.

13. That requires reflection.

14. Yes, if you are reasonable.

15. To the most frightful calamities.

16. First one, then the other.

17. That were a great calamity.

18. The least of your virtues.

THE END.

3	4	5
6	7	8
9	10	11
12	13	14
15	16	17
	18